Dropping In On...
SOUTH AFRICA

Patricia M. Moritz

A Geography Series

ROURKE CORPORATION, INC.
VERO BEACH, FLORIDA 32964

**Library of Congress
Cataloging-In-Publication Data**

Moritz, Patricia M.
South Africa/Patricia M. Moritz.
p. cm. — (Dropping in on)
Includes bibliographical references and index.
Summary: Describes some of the major cities and regions of this country located at the southern tip of the African continent.
ISBN 0-86593-493-2 (alk. paper)
1. South Africa—Juvenile literature. [1. South Africa—Description and travel.] I. Title. II. Series.
DT1719.M67   1998
968—dc21   98-15462
                                         CIP
                                          AC

South Africa

■ ■ ■ ■ ■ ■ ■ ■ ■ ■ ■ ■ ■ ■ ■

Official Name: Republic of South Africa

Area: 471,445 square miles
(1,221,040 square kilometers)

Population: 37.4 million

Capital: Pretoria

Largest City: Cape Town (pop. 854,616)

Highest Elevation: Champagne Castle,
11,072 feet (3,374 meters)

Official Languages: 11 official languages:
9 African languages, English, Afrikaans

Major Religions: Christian (30%);
Other Black Independent (17%);
Other (53%)

Money: rand

Form of Government:
Parliamentary republic

Flag:

TABLE OF CONTENTS

Our Blue Ball — The Earth

The Earth can be divided into two hemispheres. The word hemisphere means "half a ball"—in this case, the ball is the Earth.

The equator is an imaginary line that runs around the middle of the Earth. It separates the Northern Hemisphere from the Southern Hemisphere. North America— where Canada, the United States, and Mexico are located—is in the Northern Hemisphere.

The Southern Hemisphere

When the South Pole is tilted toward the sun, the sun's most powerful rays strike the southern half of the Earth and less sunshine hits the Northern Hemisphere. That is when people in the Southern Hemisphere enjoy summer. When

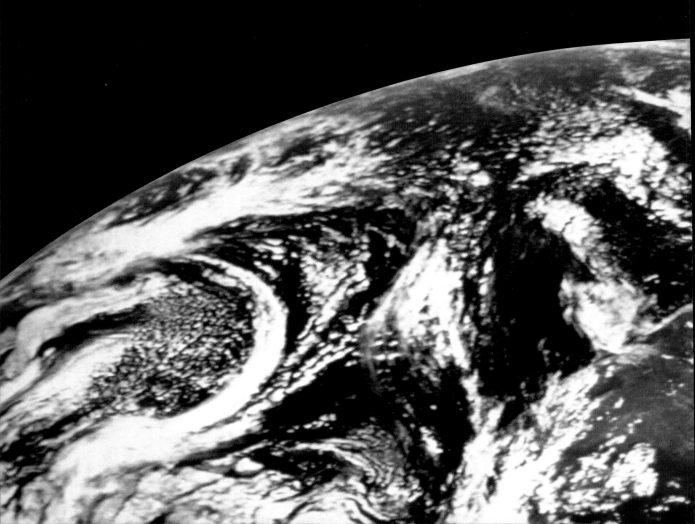

the South Pole is tilted away from the sun, and the Northern Hemisphere receives the most sunshine, the seasons reverse. Then winter comes to the Southern Hemisphere. The seasons in the Southern Hemisphere and the Northern Hemisphere are always opposite.

Get Ready for South Africa

Let's take a trip! Climb into your hot-air balloon, and we'll drop in on a country located at the southern tip of the African continent. South Africa is about three times the size of Texas and is divided into nine provinces. The "land where two oceans meet" is bordered on the east by the Indian Ocean and on the south and west by the Atlantic Ocean.

South Africa is rich in natural resources, especially gold and diamonds. It is often called the "cradle of civilization," for this is where fossils of our earliest ancestors have been discovered.

The population of South Africa includes Africans of many tribes and traditions, as well as people of European, Indian, and Asian descent.

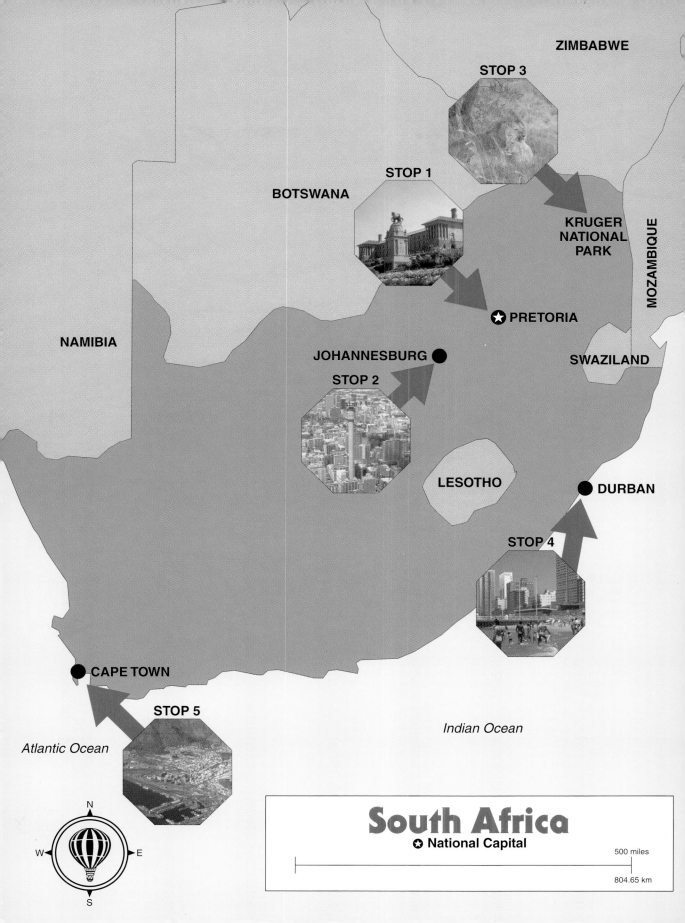

ZIMBABWE

STOP 3

STOP 1

BOTSWANA

KRUGER
NATIONAL
PARK

MOZAMBIQUE

NAMIBIA

⭐ PRETORIA

JOHANNESBURG ●

SWAZILAND

STOP 2

LESOTHO

● DURBAN

STOP 4

● CAPE TOWN

STOP 5

Indian Ocean

Atlantic Ocean

N

W ◄ ► E

S

South Africa
⭐ National Capital

500 miles
804.65 km

Stop 1: Pretoria

Our first stop will be the city of Pretoria, the administrative capital of South Africa. It is the center of political power. Most nations recognize Pretoria as the capital of South Africa. The city is located just northeast of Johannesburg in the northern province of Gauteng.

The people of Pretoria enjoy a sunny temperate climate, as is found all over South Africa. The city is known for its tree-lined streets, quiet parks, bird sanctuaries, and nature reserves. Pretoria has one of the largest zoos in the world, the National Zoological Gardens.

Pretoria is famous for its diamond mines. Several diamonds as large as baseballs have been found here.

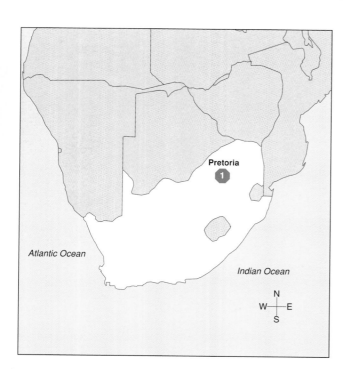

Now let's fly south-west to Johannesburg.

The president of South Africa has his office in the Union Buildings in Pretoria.

Stop 2: Johannesburg

Johannesburg is located in the northern province of Gauteng and is the largest city in South Africa. It has the tallest buildings and wealthiest neighborhoods of any city in Africa. The Nguni people call Johannesburg *iGolide*, or "City of Gold," because the city began as a gold-rush town. In 1886, gold was discovered here and is still extracted from the mines nearby. The mine shafts form honeycombs below the city's streets. Many men and women here work for the mining industry.

The Limpopo River, one of two large rivers in South Africa, begins near Johannesburg. It winds it way across the country to the Indian Ocean.

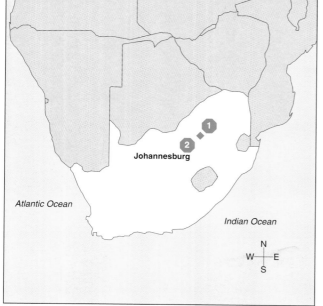

Opposite: The city of Johannesburg is the industrial center of South Africa.

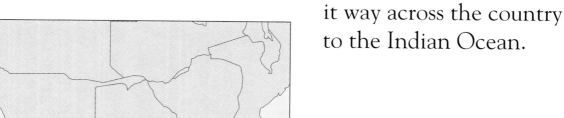

*Now we'll travel **northeast** to Kruger National Park.*

Apartheid

For many years, South Africa was ruled by white people who believed in an apartheid system of government. Apartheid means the separate and unequal development of racial groups. During apartheid, a group of townships called Soweto were set up as a place for black migrant workers to live. The people of Soweto were forced to live under poor conditions.

From the 1970's to the 1990's, the people of Soweto protested against apartheid. South Africans suffered greatly during the apartheid system. Because of apartheid, many countries of the world did not want to have any business, trade, or cultural exchanges with South Africa. South Africans were not able to participate in international sporting events, such as the Olympic Games.

South Africa became a democracy in 1994, and the apartheid system was abolished. Today, hundreds of native Africans commute everyday to their jobs in what was once "white" Johannesburg. The government and people of South Africa now look with hope to a better future.

Since becoming a democracy, the system of racial segregation in South Africa has been abolished.

Stop 3: Kruger National Park

Kruger National Park lies in the northeast region of the country called Mpumalanga. The park is about the size of the state of Massachusetts. The land here is savanna, or grassland. South Africans call it bush veld. There are many rivers and streams winding through this grassland. The combination of grass and water makes it the perfect sanctuary for wildlife.

This is the storybook Africa where wild animals roam and live just as they did hundreds of years ago. The park has some of the largest game reserves in the world. From your safari bus you can see Africa's "big five": lion, leopard, buffalo, elephant, and rhinoceros.

Now we'll travel **south** *to Durban.*

Mining in South Africa

South Africa is a treasure chest of natural resources. Diamonds are found in the remains of ancient lava. Through erosion, diamonds can be found in rivers, or even on the ocean floor. In 1866, the first diamond was found by a boy on the banks of the Orange River at Hopetown.

The largest diamond deposits are found in Kimberley where the Big Hole mine is located — the largest human-made hole in the world.

Many South Africans work in the gold mines.

The Cullinan diamond, one of the world's most famous gems.

The hole covers 38 acres (153,782 square meters), which is about the size of 20 soccer fields! The hole is 1,200 feet (365 meters) deep, which is nearly the height of the Empire State Building in New York!

Stop 4: Durban

Durban is a modern port city on the east coast of South Africa. The city lies on the Indian Ocean. The harbor here is very busy with ships from all over the world.

More than half the population of Durban is originally from India. There are more Indians living in Durban than in any city outside of India. The Indian-born lawyer Mahatma Gandhi lived in Durban for 21 years. He led a nonviolent campaign to change some anti-Indian laws.

The year-round warm climate and beautiful beaches attract many tourists to this resort city.

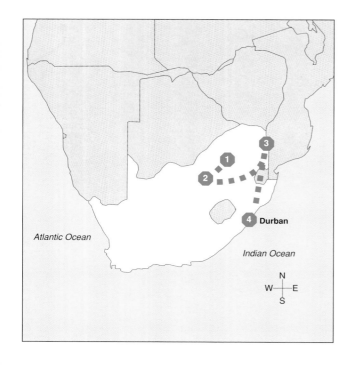

*Now let's fly **south-west** to Cape Town.*

Growing Up in South Africa

South Africa is a country of many different racial and ethnic groups, with different languages, customs, skin colors, cultures, and religions. A child in South Africa might grow up living in the countryside in a beehive-shape grass hut in a *kraal*, which is a group of houses built around a fenced area where cattle are kept. Or he or she might live in an apartment in the city.

A Ndebele kraal *in the Northern Province.*

In South Africa today, children of different races are no longer separated.

Education in South Africa is in a state of change. During apartheid, children were separated by race and sent to different schools for each racial group. Africans were not given the same quality of education as other racial groups. Schools are now integrated, but it will take some time before all children receive equal opportunities in education.

Children seven years old and older must attend school for twelve years. All South African school children wear a uniform, even in public schools. The school year begins in late January and ends in mid-December, with breaks and vacations throughout the school year.

Soccer, rugby, tennis, and swimming are popular after-school activities.

Stop 5: Cape Town

Cape Town is the law-making capital of South Africa. It is know as the "Mother City," and it is the oldest city in South Africa. The city lies on the Atlantic Ocean at the foot of majestic Table Mountain. You can take a cableway ride to the top of this famous landmark.

In 1652, the Dutch East India Company established a supply station at Cape Town to provide fresh foods to the great trading ships. Cape-Dutch manor houses are a reminder of the city's Dutch heritage.

Nearby vineyards produce some to the world's finest wines. Ostrich eggs, feathers, and meat for ostrich burgers are popular exports.

Now it's time to set sail for home.

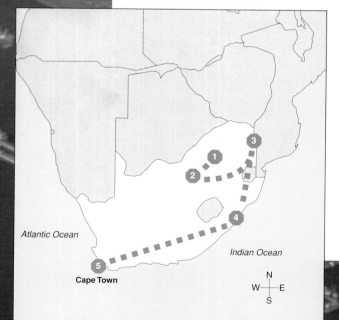

Atlantic Ocean

Indian Ocean

Cape Town

N
W — E
S

The Cape Floral Kingdom

South Africa is home to 216 of the 400 plant families found in the world.

The Cape floral kingdom occupies the southwestern corner of South Africa and a narrow strip along the southern coastline. It is the smallest but richest of the world's six floral kingdoms, and the only one found entirely within the boundaries of one country. The geography and climate of this region are unique. Over 8,000 species of flowering plants are found here.

Kirstenbosch is South Africa's national botanical gardens. It is located on the slopes of Table Mountain above Cape Town. Here you can see all the native flora of South Africa.

The most popular member of Cape flora is the protea, South Africa's national flower. Protea is named after Proteus, the Greek god who could change his shape. Like Proteus, the protea comes in a variety of forms from bushes to trees. Proteas are South Africa's top export flower.

The protea is the national flower of South Africa.

The Foods of South Africa

Traditional South African cooking combines the best foods of each of the many cultures living there over the past 300 years. The Dutch and English influences are found in the stews or *potjiekos* — meaning "little iron pot food" — sausages, and *biltong* — which is like beef jerky.

Slaves from the east, in particular Malaysia, and indentured servants from India brought spices and curries. They also added fruit to some meat dishes. The Portuguese, the first Europeans to land on the South African coast, added fish dishes. Chinese, Greeks, and Italians also have made contributions to South African recipes.

The pleasant climate of South Africa makes the *braai*—or barbecue—a favorite way of cooking. You can try unendangered game meats such as ostrich, springbok, impala, giraffe, and even crocodile.

Corn is the most popular vegetable in South African dishes—made into mealie bread, creamed, boiled, or roasted on the cob. Pumpkin and squash are also favorites.

There are many grape vineyards in South Africa.

Fruits are plentiful, with many exotic varieties such as pineapples, mangoes, and lychees available year-round. Fruit salads and baked puddings are typical South African desserts.

Glossary

apartheid   The policy of strict racial segregation and political and economic discrimination as formerly practiced in South Africa.

braai   South African barbeque.

kraal   A group of grass huts built around a fenced area where cattle are kept.

safari   A journey to see wildlife.

veld   Open grasslands with no bushes and very few trees.

Further Reading

Castello Cortes, Ian. *World Reference Atlas*. New York: Dorling Kindersley Limited, 1995.

Lauré, Jason, and Ettagale Lauré. *South Africa: Coming of Age Under Apartheid*. New York: McGraw-Hill Ryerson, Ltd., 1980.

Meisel, Jacqueline Drobis. *Exploring Cultures of the World: South Africa, a Tapestry of Peoples and Traditions*. Benchmark Books, 1997.

Palmer, John. *Guide to Places of the World*. New York: The Reader's Digest Association, Inc., 1995.

Paton, Jonathan. *The Land and People of South Africa*. New York: J.B. Lippincott, 1990.

Stein, R. Conrad. *Enchantment of the World: South Africa*. Regensteiner Publishing Enterprises, Inc., 1986.

Suggested Web Sites

Britannica Online
<http://www.info@eb.com>

Knowledge Adventure Encyclopedia
<http://www.adventure.com>

Search engine: <http://www.yahoo.com>

Index

Acknowledgments and Photo Credits
Cover: Australian Picture Library/Alan Jones/Westlight; pp. 11, 13, 15, 16, 17, 18, 19, 21 22, 23, 24–25, 27, 29: Courtesy South Africa Office of Tourism.
Maps by Paul Calderon.